RABBIT
CHASE

RABBIT CHASE

ELIZABETH LaPENSÉE KC OSTER
ANISHINAABEMOWIN TRANSLATION BY AARIN DOKUM

Cover art by KC Oster, designed by Paul Covello
Interior designed by Paul Covello
Edited by Mary Beth Leatherdale
Copyedited by Mary Ann Blair
Proofread by Mercedes Acosta

Annick Press Ltd.

We acknowledge the support of the Canada Council for the Arts and the Ontario Arts Council, and the participation of the Government of Canada/la participation du gouvernement du Canada for our publishing activities.

Library and Archives Canada Cataloguing in Publication

Title: Rabbit chase / Elizabeth LaPensée, KC Oster ; Anishinaabemowin translation by Aarin Dokum.
Names: LaPensée, Elizabeth, author. | Oster, KC, illustrator.
Identifiers: Canadiana (print) 20210328746 | Canadiana (ebook) 20210328800 | ISBN 9781773216201 (hardcover) | ISBN 9781773216195 (softcover) | ISBN 9781773216225 (PDF) | ISBN 9781773216218 (HTML)
Subjects: LCSH: Gender-nonconforming people—Juvenile fiction. | LCSH: Gender-nonconforming people—Comic books, strips, etc. | LCSH: Ojibwa Indians—Juvenile fiction. | LCSH: Ojibwa Indians—Comic books, strips, etc. | LCGFT: Comics (Graphic works) | LCGFT: Graphic novels.
Classification: LCC PN6727.L37 R33 2022 | DDC j741.5/973—dc23

Published in the U.S.A. by Annick Press (U.S.) Ltd.
Distributed in Canada by University of Toronto Press.
Distributed in the U.S.A. by Publishers Group West.

Printed in Canada

annickpress.com
elizabethlapensee.com
kcpawz.com

Also available as an e-book. Please visit annickpress.com/ebooks for more details.

Rabbit Chase was written with gratitude to Shannon Martin for her part in restoring gatherings at the Sanilac Petroglyphs. For my grandparents, who have seen the damage done to the petroglyphs and hold onto memories of when they felt comfort walking there together. For my mama, who filled me up with love. For my children, who carry on hope in their very being, expressing themselves as they are.

—E. L.

All of the author's earnings are donated to the Sanilac Petroglyphs for their protection and recognition.

To my friends and family who believed in me and my passions. And to the youth reading this today; know that I believe in you too.

—K.C. O.

TRANSLATIONS

aambe – come on, come here

Aaniish go naa aapji?! – Jeez! / What in the world?! / What on earth?!

Baamaapii ka waamin – See you later

baashknjibgwaan – trillium

Boozhoo – Greetings!

deminan – strawberries

ehn – yes

Jiibayaabooz (Jee-bye-ah-bows) – one of the Trickster brothers. He guides those who have passed on home along the Path of Spirits, the Milky Way.

makade-aaboo – coffee (black water)

miigwech – thanks, thank you

miinan – blueberries

minwaa – and/also

mnoomin – wild rice

mskwaabik – copper (red metal)

Nanaboozhoo (Na-na-bow-zhoo) – the best known of the Trickster brothers. He often gets into trouble of his own making.

Nbagminaandam – I am becoming hungry.

Ngiisaadendam – I am sorry. / I feel regret. / I am sad.

niikaane – my older brother

Paayehnsag – Little People, water spirits, rock spirits

shtaahaa – wow!

zgime'ig – mosquitoes

zhaagnaashag – white people

ziiwaagmide – maple syrup

zinaakobiiganan – petroglyphs

CHAPTER 1
THE FIELD TRIP
ALL STAFF, STUDENTS, AND TEACHERS OF THE INDIGENOUS STUDENTS ASSOCIATION REPORT TO THE BUS FOR THE FIELD TRIP TO THE PETROGLYPHS.
LOOK WHO DOESN'T HAVE ANY FRIENDS TO GO WITH HER.
AIMÉE'S NOT ALONE. SHE SAYS SHE'S *THEY/THEM.*
HOW'S THAT WORK ANYWAY?
ZHAAGNAASHAG...
DID SHE FORGET SHE WAS BORN A GIRL?
HAHA!

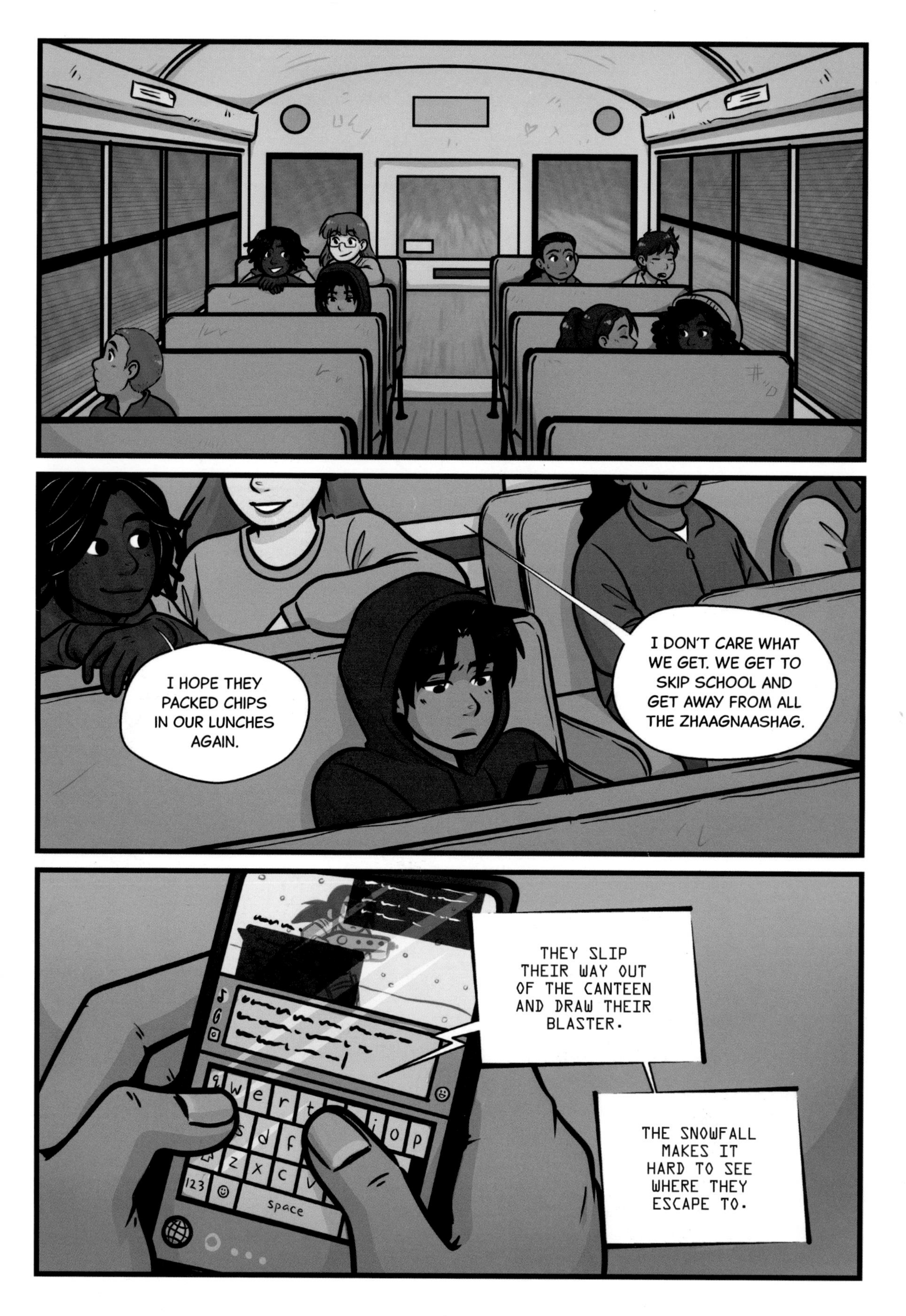
I HOPE THEY PACKED CHIPS IN OUR LUNCHES AGAIN.
I DON'T CARE WHAT WE GET. WE GET TO SKIP SCHOOL AND GET AWAY FROM ALL THE ZHAAGNAASHAG.
THEY SLIP THEIR WAY OUT OF THE CANTEEN AND DRAW THEIR BLASTER.
THE SNOWFALL MAKES IT HARD TO SEE WHERE THEY ESCAPE TO.

WE'RE HERE! PLEASE PUT AWAY ALL YOUR DEVICES!
FINALLY! FEELS GOOD TO STRETCH!
WOULD'VE FELT FASTER IF I HAD BROUGHT MY PHONE LIKE AIMÉE.
UGH. I WAS SO CLOSE TO FINDING THE TARGET...
FOUND THEM! JUST GOTTA BE SMART WITH THIS ATTACK.

AAMBE! COME ON, AIMÉE!
PUT YOUR PHONE AWAY!
JUST A SEC!
YOU'LL ALWAYS HAVE YOUR PHONE. YOU WON'T ALWAYS BE YOUNG ENOUGH FOR THIS CEREMONY.
BUT I WON'T EVER BE ON THIS MISSION AGAIN!
BOOZHOO.

THAT COPPER IS SO JAGGED. WHAT CAN THEY USE THAT FOR?
PAAYEHNSAG HAVE ALL THE TOOLS AND KNOWLEDGE THEY NEED TO MELT AND SHAPE MSKWAABIK.
HAHA!
HAHA!
THEY EVEN HAVE ENGINEERS WITH MECHANICAL SKILLS.

WE KNOW PAAYEHNSAG—WHICH ARE ALSO CALLED WATER SPIRITS, ROCK SPIRITS, OR LITTLE PEOPLE—LIKE OFFERINGS OF COPPER AND MNOOMIN BY ZINAAKOBIIGANAN.

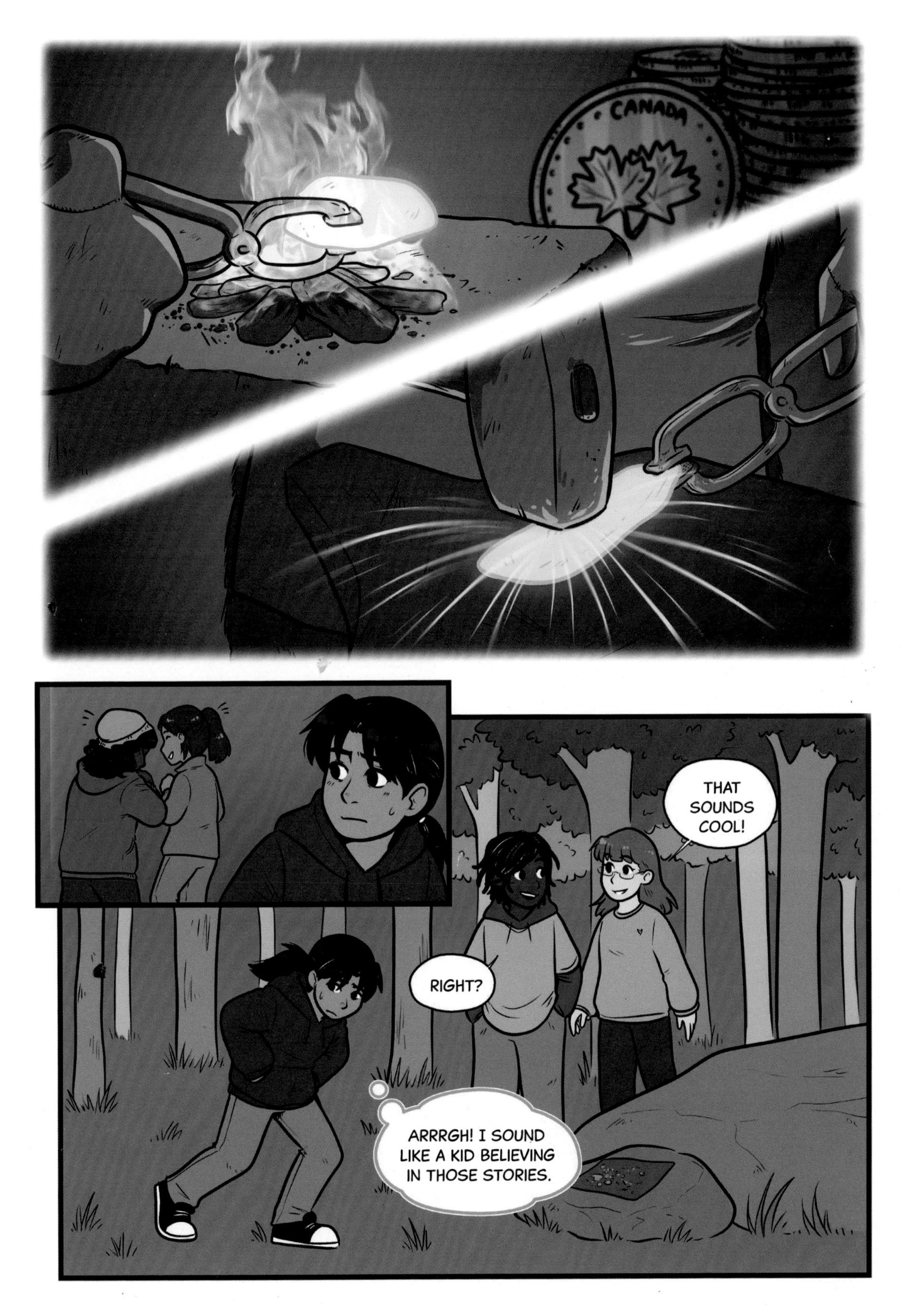
CANADA
THAT SOUNDS COOL!
RIGHT?
ARRRGH! I SOUND LIKE A KID BELIEVING IN THOSE STORIES.

ONLY YOUTH ARE TRUSTED BY PAAYEHNSAG.
SO YOU'LL MAKE OFFERINGS ON YOUR OWN.
LOOK OUT FOR ONE ANOTHER!

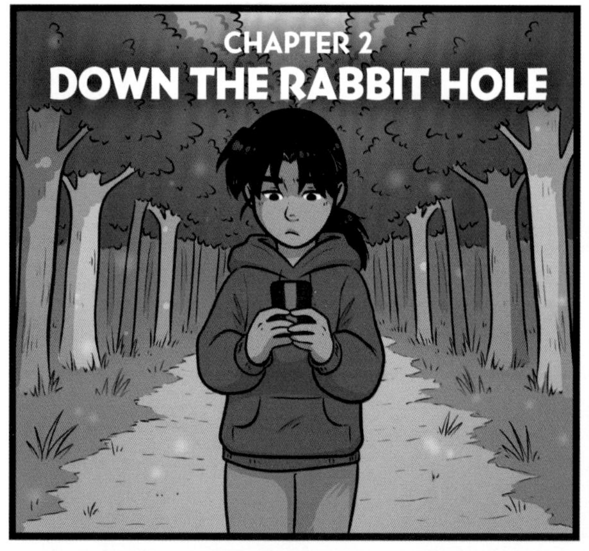
CHAPTER 2
DOWN THE RABBIT HOLE

NO CONNECTION

WEIRD...

HAVE YOU PERHAPS DIED?
UHHH...
AM I DEAD? MY CONNECTION IS...
NOT DEAD? THEN YOU'RE NOT MY PROBLEM, GIRL.
I WISH EVERYONE WOULD STOP CALLING ME A GIRL.
WHAT AM I SUPPOSED TO CALL YOU THEN?

HOW DID YOU... DID YOU READ MY MIND?
NOT SURPRISED HE DOESN'T KNOW THAT IN MY LANGUAGE SOME PRONOUNS CAN BE GENDER NEUTRAL.
YOUR LANGUAGE? BUT DON'T WE ALL SPEAK ANISHNAABEMOWIN HERE?
YOU SHOULD LEARN TO KEEP YOUR THOUGHTS TO YOURSELF.
WHERE IS *HERE*?
EVERYWHERE AND NOWHERE. AT LEAST IT WILL BE NOWHERE IF WE CAN'T STOP OUR LAND FROM BEING SIGNED AWAY.
WAIT! WHERE AM I?
VERY BUSY! VERY BUSY!
GREAT... CAN'T EVEN KEEP UP WITH A MIND READING RABBIT.

WHAT IS THIS PLACE?
THIS PLACE IS HERE, I SUPPOSE.
I AM ALWAYS RIGHT WHERE I AM.

AT LEAST WHEN I DIE, I'LL BE THAT RABBIT'S PROBLEM AND THEN HE'LL HAVE TO HELP ME...

SHE WON'T LISTEN IN CLASS AND FORGETS HER HOMEWORK.
THEY'RE STRUGGLING BECAUSE *THEY* DON'T FEEL ACCEPTED IN YOUR CLASSROOM.
RIGHT... THAT *GENDER* STUFF.

ZINAAKOBIIGANAN ARE NEAR THE RIVER. SO I SHOULD BE ABLE TO FOLLOW THE WATER BACK.
IT'S SO LATE. THEY PROBABLY WENT BACK WITHOUT ME...

CHAPTER 3:
THE VISITORS
WELL LOOK WHAT ZGIME'IG DRAGGED IN!
WITH NO HELP FROM YOU, JIIBAYAABOOZ.
LOOKS LIKE YOU GOT HELP FROM PAAYEHNSAG THOUGH.

THOSE CLEVER LITTLE WATER SPIRITS ARE RARELY SEEN.

ALTHOUGH THEY WILL COME OUT FOR SWEETS.
SWEET

MISCHIEF IS CERTAINLY THEIR MODE OF CHOICE.

EXCEPT WHEN THEY HELP CHILDREN. DID YOU HEAR THE ONE ABOUT THE BABIES LOST IN THE BUSH WHO SURVIVED THE NIGHT?
IT WAS PAAYEHNSAG, I TELL YOU!

I KNOW THE STORIES.
AND I'M NOT A CHILD.
ON THE CONTRARY. IF YOU WEREN'T THEY WOULDN'T BE HELPING YOU.
EITHER WAY, SINCE YOU'RE ALIVE, WE MAY BE ABLE TO MAKE A TRADE.
WHAT KIND OF TRADE?
THE TRADE BEGINS WITH A STORY.

I, JIIBAYAABOOZ, WALKED THE PATH HOME . . .
AND NOW SHOW THE DEAD THE WAY.

BUT I STILL HAVE
ENEMIES WHO DWELL
IN THE DARK WATERS.

ONLY THE
PAAYEHNSAG,
WITH THEIR STONE
CANOES THAT CUT
THROUGH THE WATER,
CAN BRING ME
VENGEANCE . . .

AND PUT AN END
TO THE SPIRITS THAT
PULLED ME UNDER.

WAIT, WAIT, WAIT.
AM I SUPPOSED TO FIGHT WATER SPIRITS TO GET HOME?
I'M OUT!
AS IF YOU COULD! I NEED YOU TO CONVINCE PAAYEHNSAG TO HELP ME.
I KNOW YOU KNOW ABOUT MAKING OFFERINGS.
YOU SEE, ONLY PAAYEHNSAG KNOW WHERE THOSE SPIRITS ARE HIDING SINCE THEY SHARE THE WATERS.
AND THEY WON'T TALK TO ME. BUT THEY WILL TALK TO A CHILD... LIKE YOU.

UGH. I'M NOT A CHILD.
WHAT ELSE DO YOU SUPPOSE YOU ARE?
RIGHT THEN. YOU WILL NEED TO FOLLOW THE PATH OF STARS NOT OF SPACE TO THE PLACE NEAR WATER WHERE STONE AND GROUND BECOME AIR.
I DIDN'T SAY I WAS GOING TO HELP YOU.
AND I DON'T EVEN KNOW WHAT THAT MEANS.
HOLD ONTO THESE AS AN OFFERING FOR PAAYEHNSAG.
AND PRACTICE NOT THINKING SO LOUDLY.
KEEP UP!

WHAT A JOKE.
IF HE WAS REALLY GOING TO HELP, HE WOULDN'T TAKE OFF.
I SHOULDN'T HAVE TO EARN MY WAY HOME.

I CAN FIND IT ON MY OWN.

CHAPTER 4
INTO THE WOODS

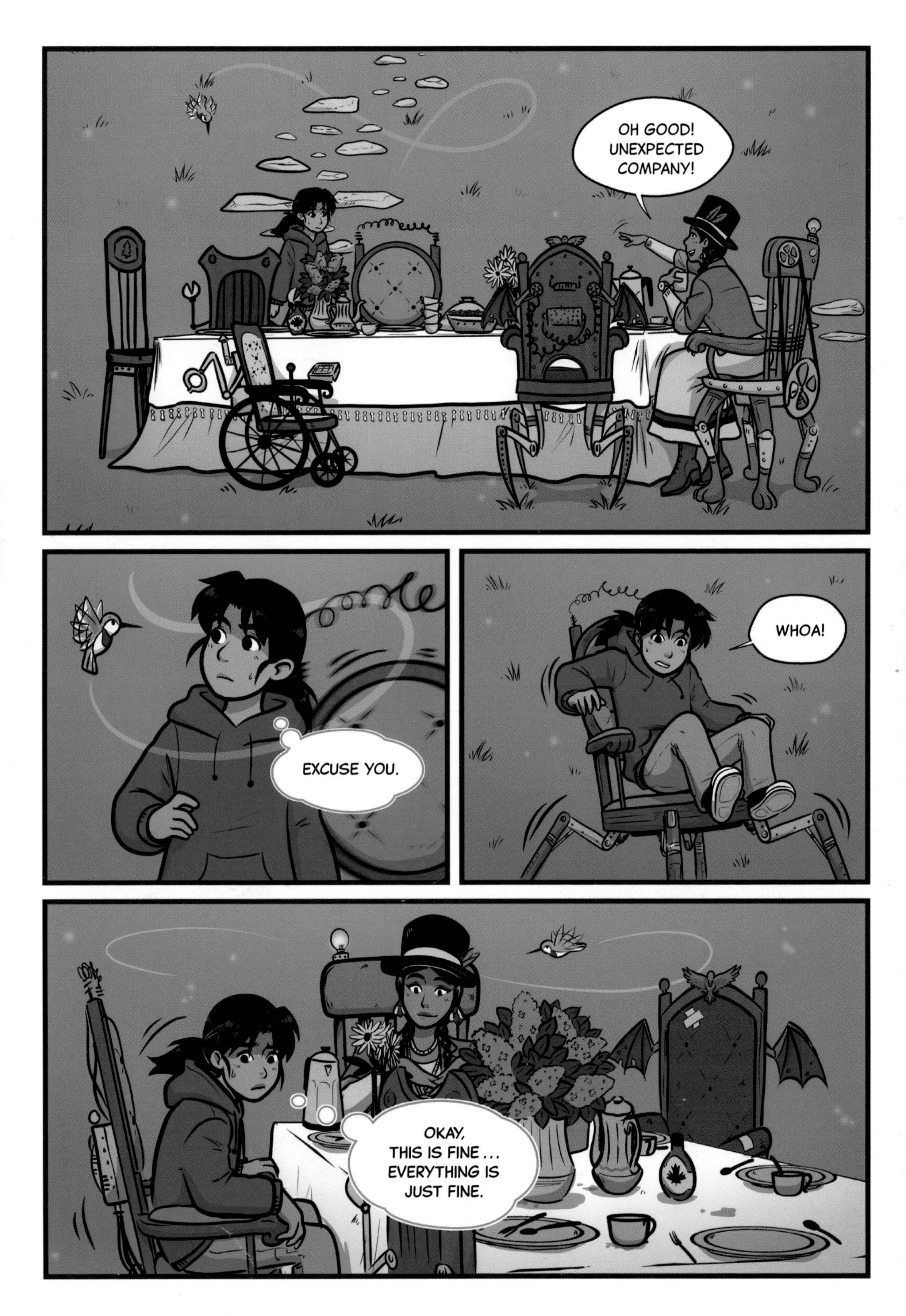
OH GOOD! UNEXPECTED COMPANY!
EXCUSE YOU.
WHOA!
OKAY, THIS IS FINE . . . EVERYTHING IS JUST FINE.

MMM.
LIKE WHEN MOM MAKES BREAKFAST FOR DINNER.
WOULD YOU LIKE COFFEE WITH YOUR MAPLE SYRUP?
IF OUR GUEST OF HONOR DOESN'T WANT MAPLE SYRUP, I CALL IT!
UMMM...
HONOR?
MMM, MAKADE-AABOO.

NANABOOZHOO!
NANABOOZHOO? THE TRICKSTER?
DON'T MIND IF I DO.
WOW. HE'S REALLY REAL...
SO GOOD OF YOU TO JOIN US. AND OUR GUEST OF HONOR!
OH, MY NAME IS AIMÉE.
WELCOME, GUEST OF HONOR!
WELCOME, AIMÉE!
WELCOME, AIMÉE!
WELCOME, AIMÉE!

HAVE YOU SEEN WHAT THE QUEEN DID TO THE SWAMP?
DRAINED IT AND FLATTENED IT, SHE DID!
SHE'LL SURELY COME FOR YOUR LAND TOO, AUNTIE!
SHE SENT PAPERS, BUT I REFUSE TO SIGN!
THAT WON'T STOP THE THE QUEEN . . .

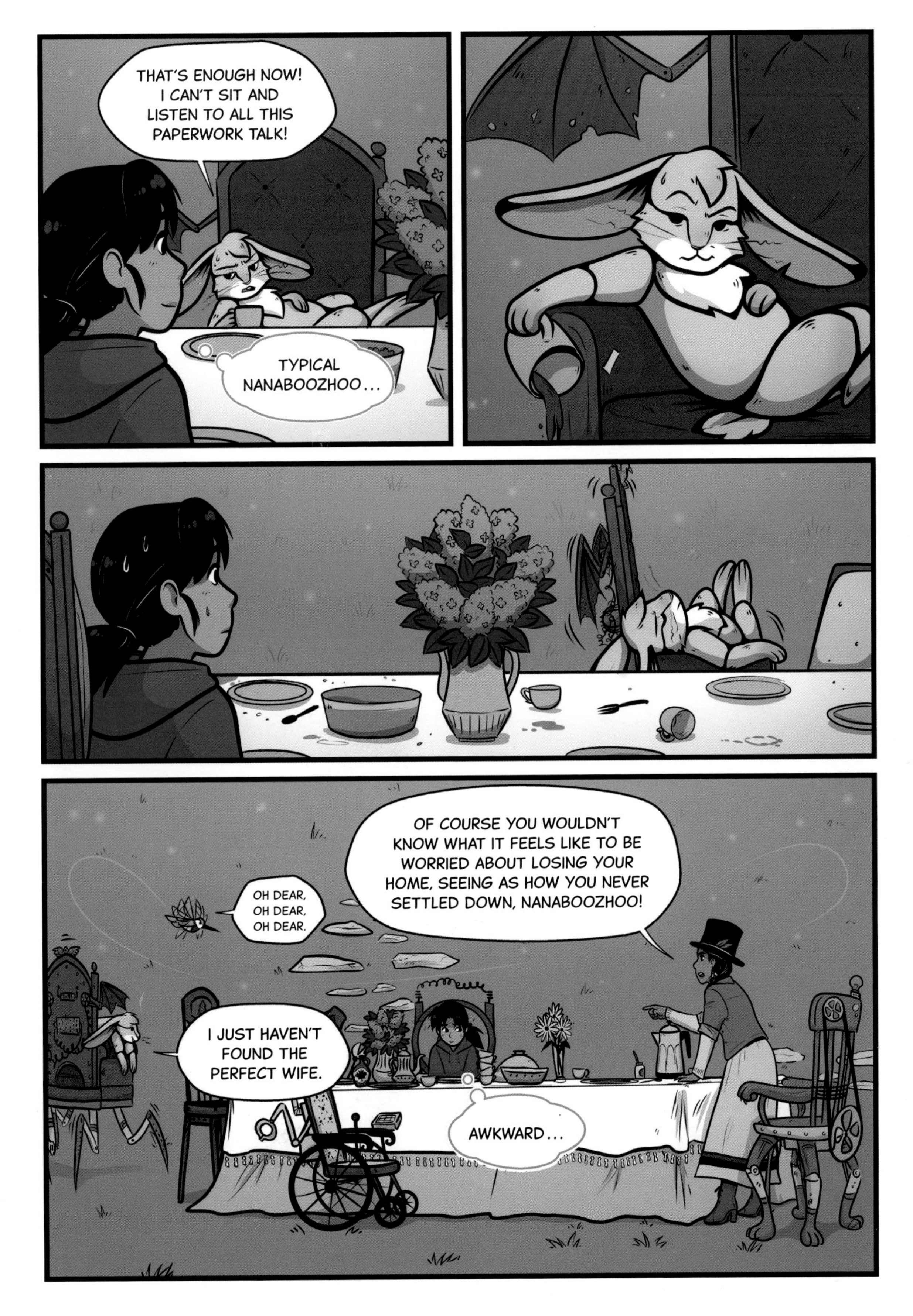
THAT'S ENOUGH NOW! I CAN'T SIT AND LISTEN TO ALL THIS PAPERWORK TALK!
TYPICAL NANABOOZHOO...
OF COURSE YOU WOULDN'T KNOW WHAT IT FEELS LIKE TO BE WORRIED ABOUT LOSING YOUR HOME, SEEING AS HOW YOU NEVER SETTLED DOWN, NANABOOZHOO!
OH DEAR, OH DEAR, OH DEAR.
I JUST HAVEN'T FOUND THE PERFECT WIFE.
AWKWARD...

YOU KNOW, I REALLY SHOULD BE GOING NOW.
OH REALLY? WHERE TO? WHAT COULD BE MORE IMPORTANT THAN MIINAN?
MINWAA ZIIWAAGMIDE?
NEVER YOU MIND THE MESS. YOU ARE A GUEST!
I HAVE TO GET HOME. EVEN WITHOUT THE WHITE RABBIT.
JIIBAYAABOOZ...

CHAPTER 5
TEA GOSSIP
YOU KNOW HIM?
NIIKAANE. TRUE STORY.
OHHH. THE TRICKSTER BROTHERS.
I RARELY SEE HIM ANYMORE. HE'S ALWAYS BUSY DOING MORE IMPORTANT THINGS THAN GOSSIPING OVER TEA.
BUT GOSSIPING IS ONE OF THE MOST IMPORTANT THINGS WE DO!
IT SAVES LIVES, IT DOES!
TRULY!
THAT'S WHAT I SAID!

MAYBE I SHOULD HELP JIIBAYAABOOZ?
I REALLY DO NEED TO BE GOING.
OH, BUT AIMÉE, IT'S GETTING SO DARK. IT WILL BE COLD OUT THERE.
SURELY LOTS OF CREEPY CRAWLY THINGS WILL BE OUT AND ABOUT!
YOU SHOULD STAY AT MY HOME FOR THE NIGHT AND GET A GOOD REST!
IT'S TRUE I HAVEN'T HAD MUCH SLEEP...
THERE NEVER WAS A TRUER STORY TOLD!

UHHH... HELP?
MIIGWECH FOR THE STORIES AND THE TEA. BAAMAAPII KA WAAMIN.
LOVELY VISITING WITH YOU, NANABOOZHOO. YOU ARE ALWAYS WELCOME TO MY TEA AND BERRIES.

THIS IS SO BEAUTIFUL!
I JUST HOPE THE QUEEN DOESN'T TRY TO TAKE THE STARS FROM ME TOO.
I HOPE YOU HAVE A GOOD SLEEP.
AND WHATEVER YOU DO, DON'T BLOW OUT THE LIGHT.

WHAT OFFERINGS HAVE YOU BROUGHT?
NOTHING REALLY, BUT NBAGMINAANDAM!
IT WOULD HAVE BEEN POLITE TO BRING FOOD TO SHARE.
NOW WHAT WOULD BE THE POINT OF THAT?

SINCE YOU ARE A GUEST, I WILL COOK FOR YOU AND LEAVE THIS LIGHT FOR YOU.
WHATEVER YOU DO. DON'T LET THE LIGHT GO OUT.

THIS IS IMPOSSIBLE...
I JUST WANT TO BE HOME AND ASLEEP.

CHAPTER 6
GROWING PAINS
CREAK
CRACK

WHY WON'T YOU JUST LISTEN TO WHAT YOU'RE TOLD?!
YOU KNOW THAT YOU KNOW BETTER!
I-I DIDN'T KNOW, AUNTIE...
WHAT DID I DO?
I DIDN'T MEAN TO...
I GUESS HELPING JIIBAYAABOOZ REALLY IS MY ONLY CHANCE AT GETTING HOME.

IF I CAN'T FIND THE WAY TO THE PAAYEHNSAG, I'LL NEVER FIND MY WAY HOME.
THAT HURTS, YOU KNOW.

PARDON ME, YOU ARE STANDING ON MY ROOTS.
OH, I'M SORRY! I DIDN'T REALIZE . . .
YOUR KIND RARELY DO!
OH NO, THE SUN ISN'T HIGH.
IT'S SO COLD . . .

HERE YOU GO, DEMINAN.
OH, MIIGWECH!
MIIGWECH!
WHAT STRANGE FOLIAGE.
SUCH DULL COLORS.
THEY LOOK LOVELY, ACTUALLY.
AND YOUR NAME IS?

MY MOM
NAMED ME
AIMÉE.
DOES THAT
NAME MAKE
YOU SAD?
IT'S NOT
THAT...
IT'S THAT
I'LL NEVER SEE
MY MOM AGAIN
IF I DON'T FIND THE
PAAYEHNSAG.

WE KNOW WHERE TO FIND THEM!
WE CAN HELP!
SHHH!
AIMÉE IS A CHILD. PAAYEHNSAG WILL BE SAFE.

MIIGWECH, BAASHKNJIBGWAAN. HOW CAN I FIND THEM?

WE, THE PLANT PEOPLE, ARE VERY GOOD FRIENDS WITH THE WATER SPIRITS.
PAAYEHNSAG EVEN SAVED THE LIVES OF OUR LITTLE STRAWBERRIES.
OUR LITTLE STRAWBERRIES GROW NATURALLY...

THE QUEEN DETESTED THEM SIMPLY BECAUSE SHE HAD NO CONTROL OVER THEM.
AND SO THEY HAD TO BE CARRIED BY PAAYEHNSAG TO SAFETY.
AS THANKS FOR CARING FOR OUR LITTLE STRAWBERRIES, WE ARE HAPPY TO INTRODUCE YOU TO OUR CARETAKERS.
THAT WOULD MAKE JIIBAYAABOOZ HAPPY.

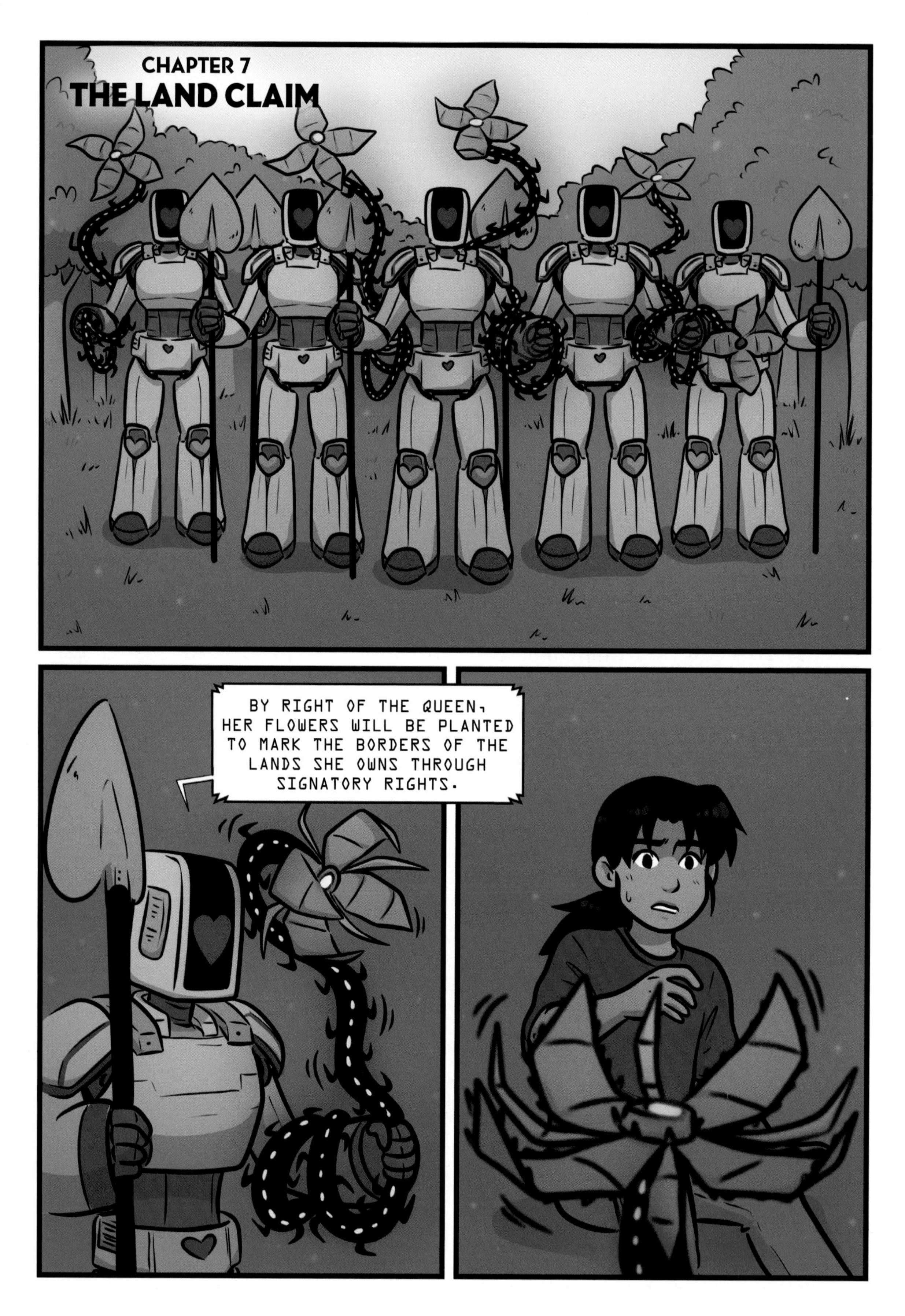
CHAPTER 7
THE LAND CLAIM
BY RIGHT OF THE QUEEN, HER FLOWERS WILL BE PLANTED TO MARK THE BORDERS OF THE LANDS SHE OWNS THROUGH SIGNATORY RIGHTS.

Social Studies: Christopher Columbus
pg 87 Q 1-10
pg 89 Q 14-16
DON'T FORGET, YOUR REFLECTION ON THE VOYAGE OF DISCOVERY IS DUE TOMORROW.
COLUMBUS DIDN'T DISCOVER AMERICA.
OH, YEAH, WHATEVER YOU SAY.
pew
IF I COULD SPACETIME TRAVEL, I'D STOP HIM BEFORE HE EVEN GOT HERE.

HEY AIMÉE...
WHAT ARE YOU GONNA DO ABOUT COLUMBUS NOW?

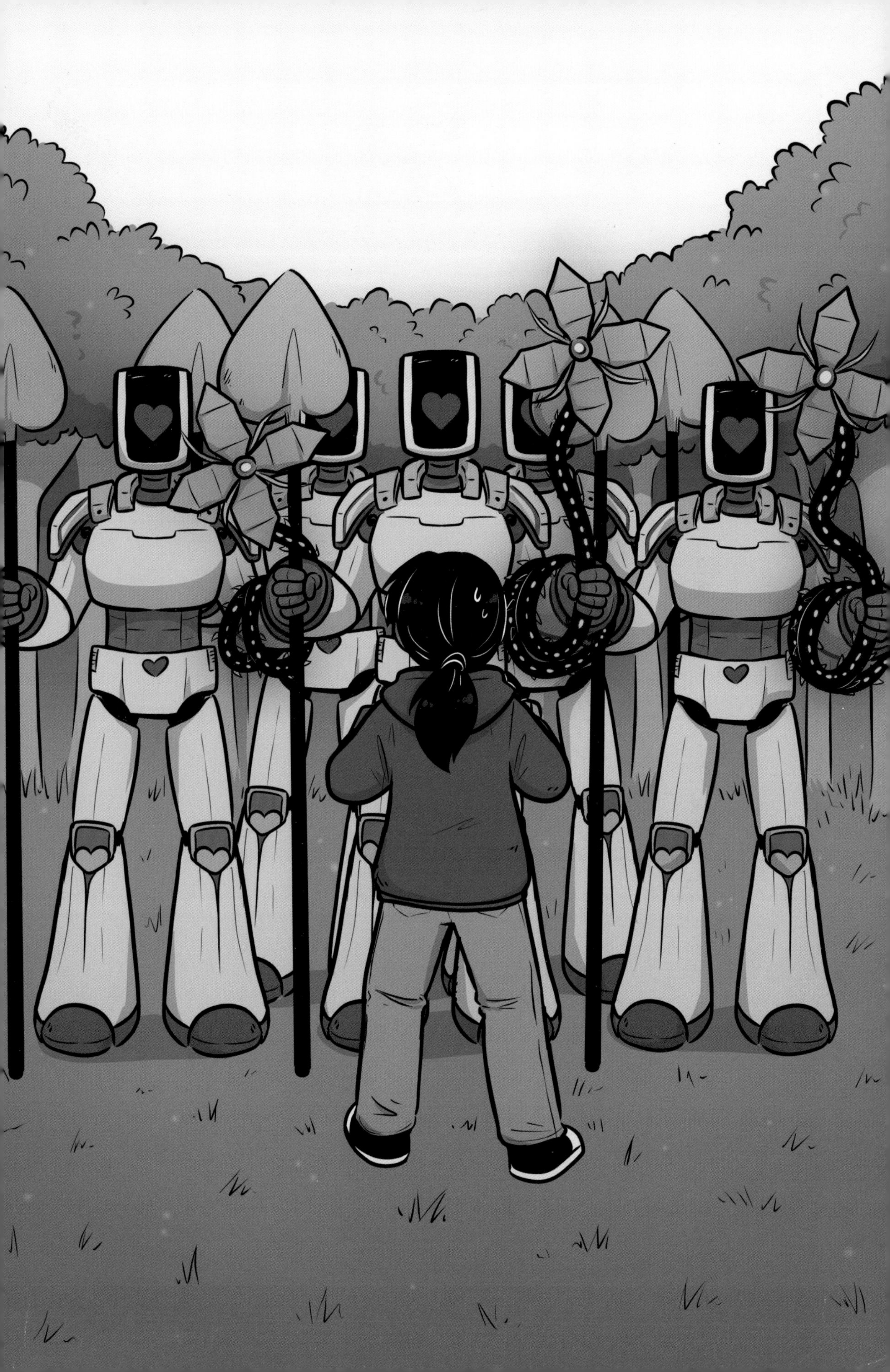

WATCH OUT!

WHY DON'T YOU PICK ON SOMEONE YOUR OWN SIZE!
OH, BUT DEAR, THEY'RE QUITE A BIT BIGGER THAN EVEN YOU!

YOU SHOULDN'T PICK ON FLOWERS!
UH-OH...

THAT WAS WAY
TOO CLOSE!

^#*!

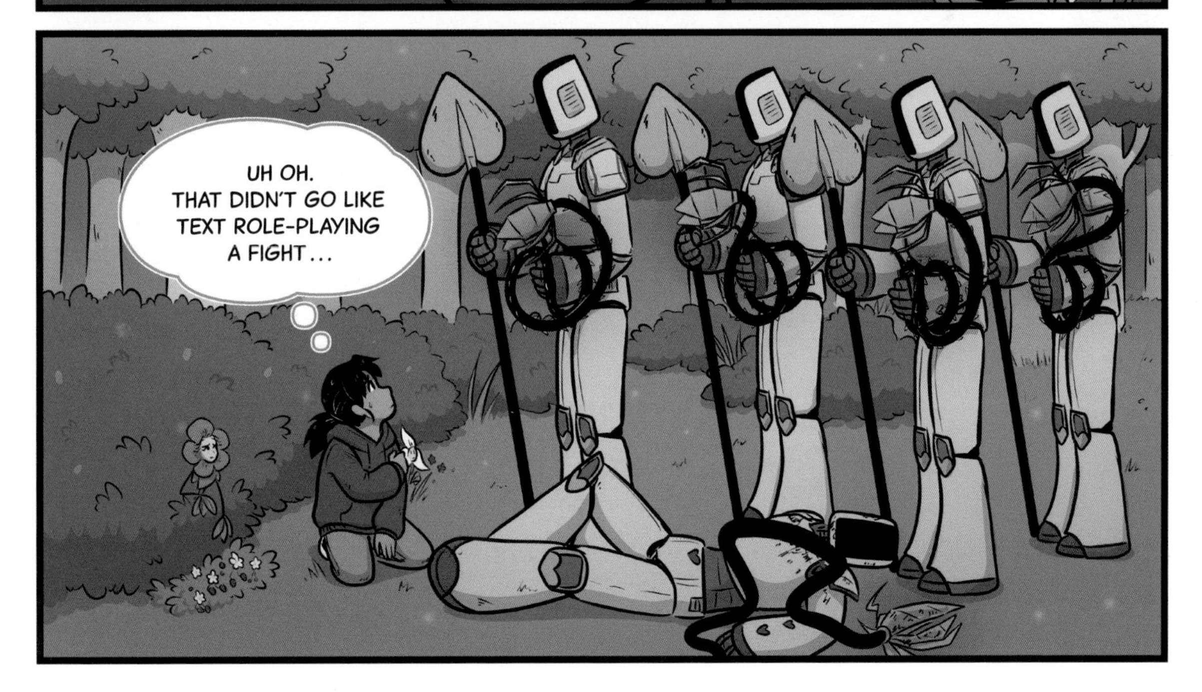
UH OH.
THAT DIDN'T GO LIKE
TEXT ROLE-PLAYING
A FIGHT...

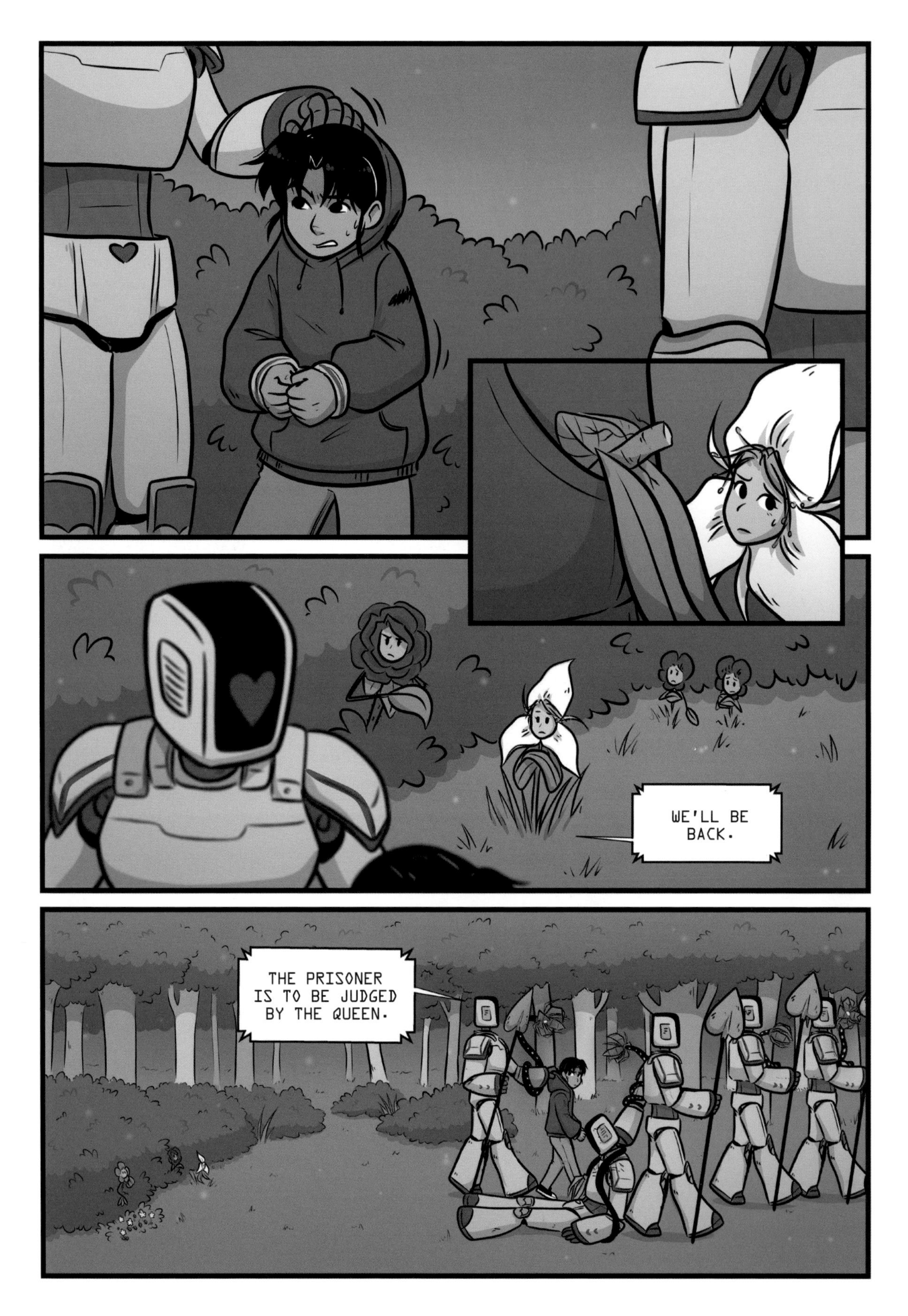
WE'LL BE BACK.
THE PRISONER IS TO BE JUDGED BY THE QUEEN.

CHAPTER 8
THE QUEEN'S COURT

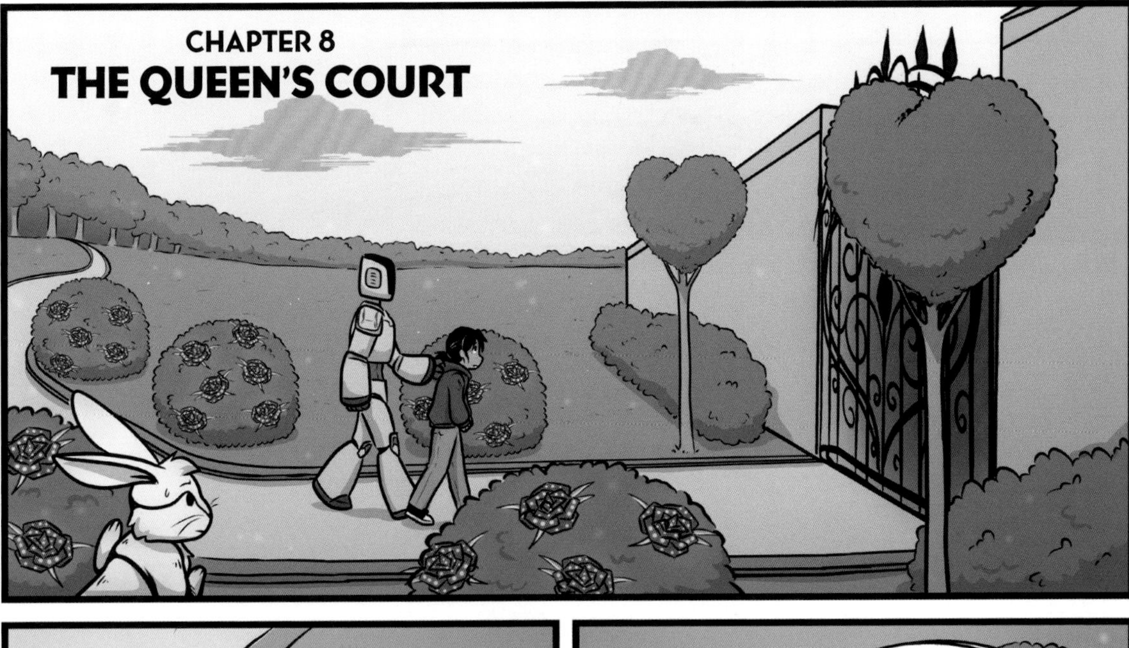

COME ON NOW, WE HAVE TO GET GOING!
IT'S FINE. THEY'RE GONE.

WHAT'S THIS?!

GONE

WHO, OR RATHER *WHAT*, ARE YOU?
ARE YOU A LITTLE BOY? A GIRL?

A GAMER.
OH, YOU PLAY GAMES, DO YOU? I DO SO LOVE GAMES.
WHY DON'T WE PLAY A GAME?

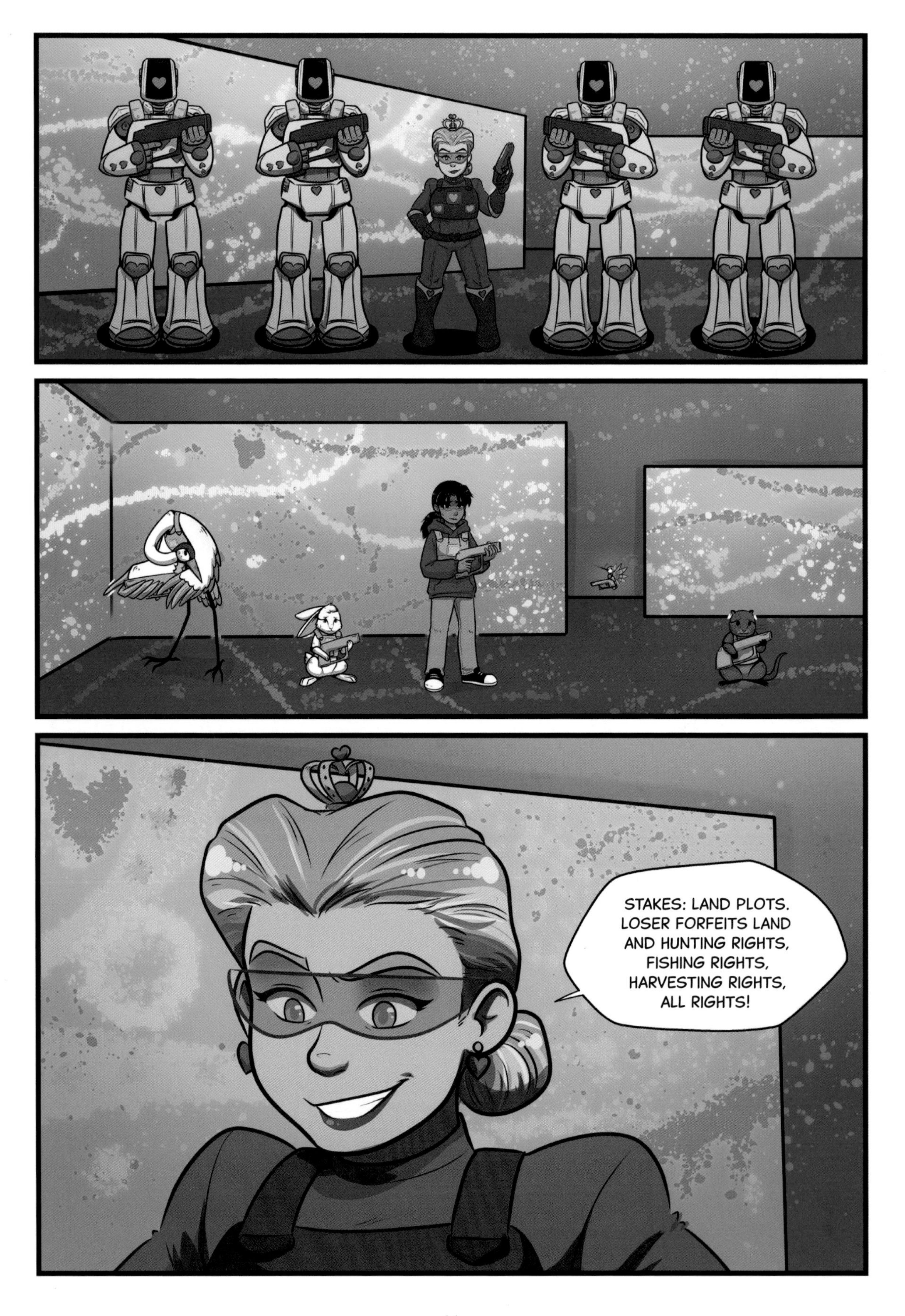
STAKES: LAND PLOTS. LOSER FORFEITS LAND AND HUNTING RIGHTS, FISHING RIGHTS, HARVESTING RIGHTS, ALL RIGHTS!

IF WE DON'T WIN, IT'LL BE MY FAULT THEY LOSE THEIR LAND...
QUEEN
MISFITS
3
0
WELL, WELL, WELL. I ALREADY OWN THE RIVER WHERE YOU MET YOUR FATE, JIIBAYAABOOZ.
NOW I'LL OWN WHAT LITTLE LAND YOU HAVE LEFT.
PEW
CLICK
CLICK
AND YOUR BROTHER'S LAND TOO!

THIS GAME HAS TO BE RIGGED!
AANIISH GO NAA AAPJI?!
SEE? IT DIDN'T EVEN FIRE.
CLICK

COME OUT, COME OUT, WHEREVER YOU ARE...

COMING TO GET YOU...

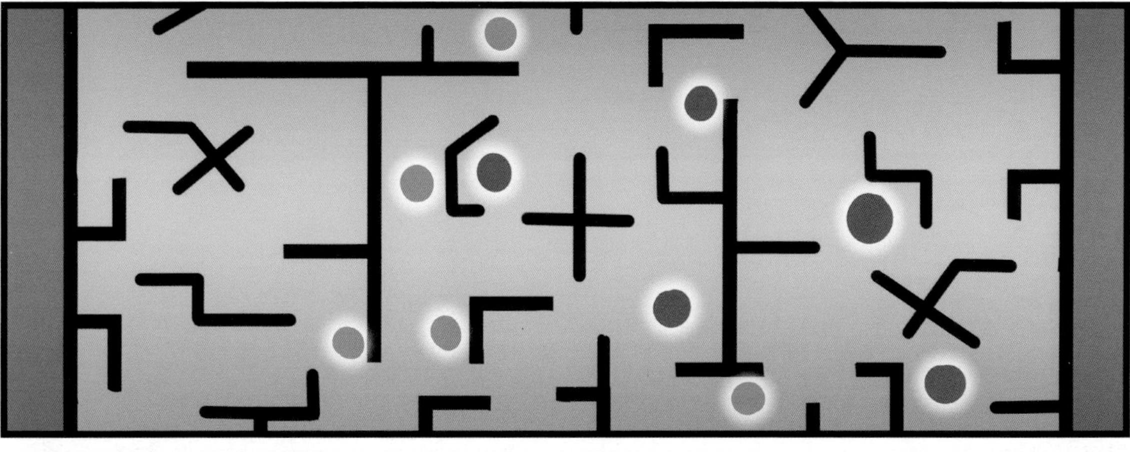

CLICK
PEW

PEW
CLICK

QUEEN
5
MISFITS
4
I ADVISE LETTING THE QUEEN WIN IF YOU DON'T WANT TROUBLE.
BUT I'M BETTER THAN HER.
SIGH
CLICK
PEW

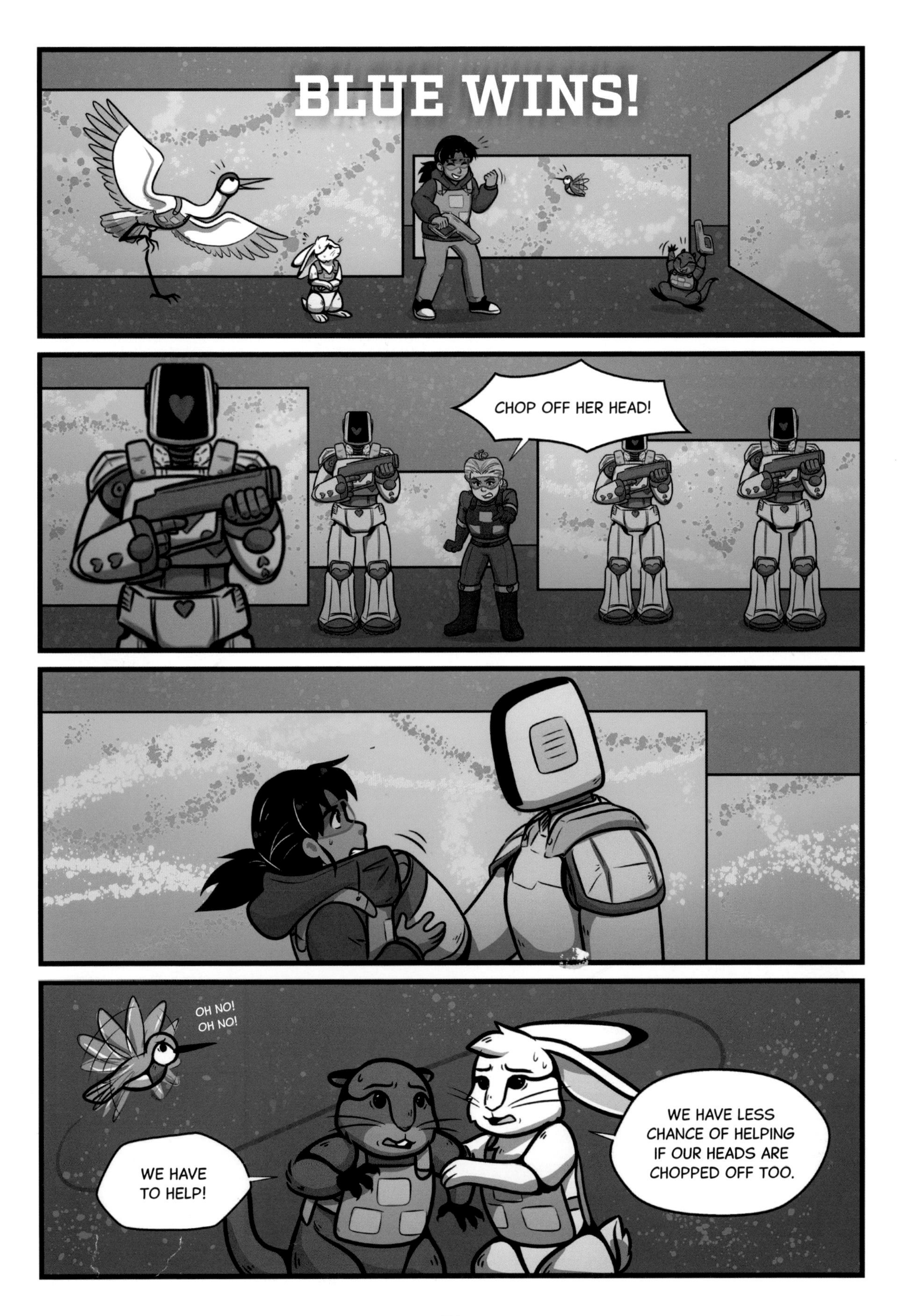
BLUE WINS!
CHOP OFF HER HEAD!
OH NO!
OH NO!
WE HAVE TO HELP!
WE HAVE LESS CHANCE OF HELPING IF OUR HEADS ARE CHOPPED OFF TOO.

CHAPTER 9
THE TRIAL
I OWN MORE LAND THAN YOU'LL EVER SEE.
AND I'LL HAVE YOUR HEAD TOO.
NO ONE DEFEATS THE QUEEN!

FIRST WITNESS!
AUNTIE!
NGIISAADENDAM, BUT WITH THE POOR STATE MY HOUSE IS IN, THE QUEEN THREATENS TO HAVE IT CONDEMNED.
THEN SHE CAN CLAIM IT AS LAND.
TO THE STAND OR YOU'LL ALL LOSE YOUR HEADS!

YES, YOUR MAJESTY. THE PERSON IN QUESTION DID DESTROY MY HOME.
WOULD YOU, IN FACT, CALL THIS PERSON CARELESS?
I DIDN'T KNOW WHAT WOULD HAPPEN!
SILENCE! ORDER IN THE COURT!
WOULD YOU SAY THAT THIS PERSON'S HEAD IS SO BIG THAT THEY BURST YOUR HOME?
Y-Y-YES.

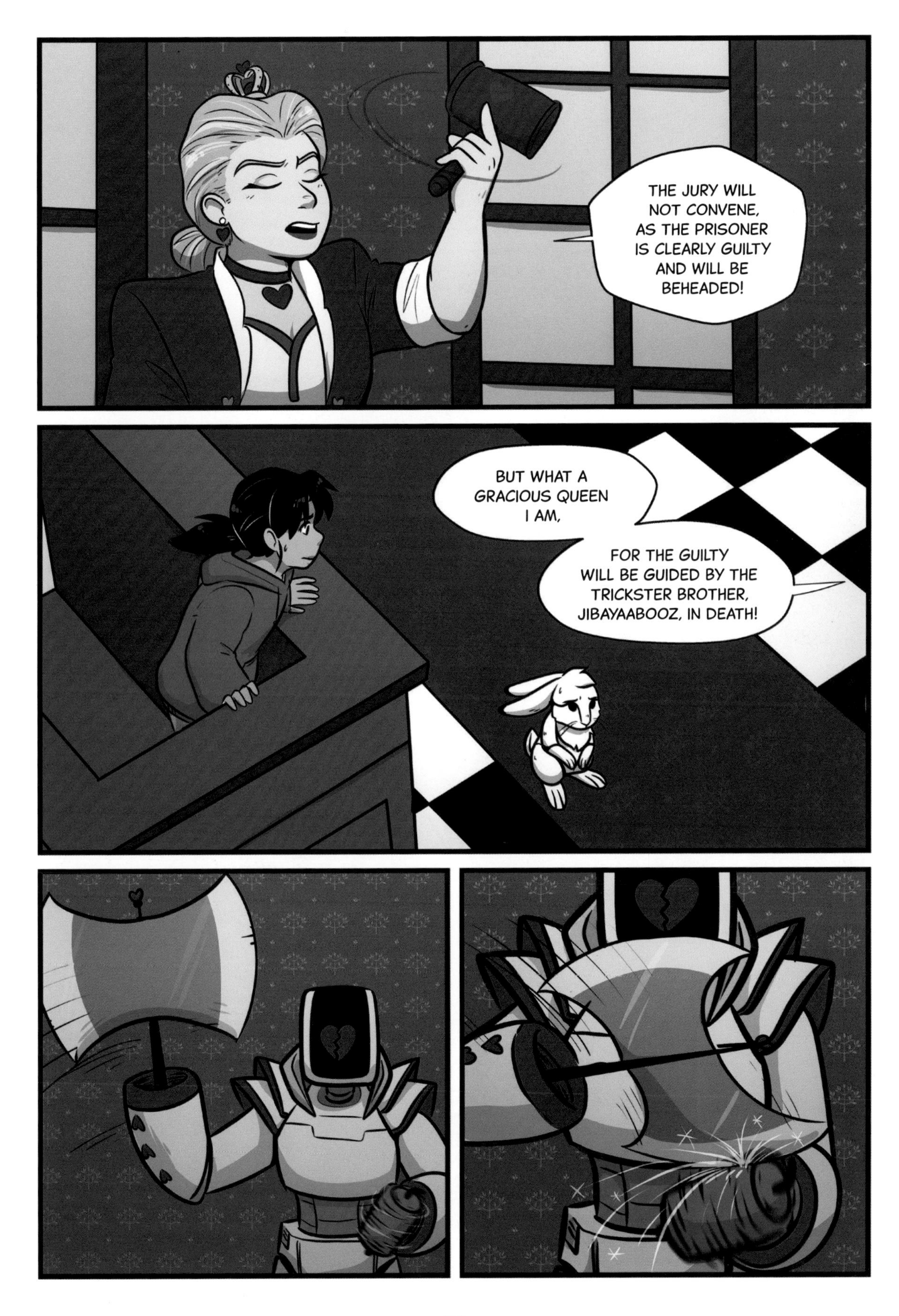
THE JURY WILL NOT CONVENE, AS THE PRISONER IS CLEARLY GUILTY AND WILL BE BEHEADED!
BUT WHAT A GRACIOUS QUEEN I AM,
FOR THE GUILTY WILL BE GUIDED BY THE TRICKSTER BROTHER, JIBAYAABOOZ, IN DEATH!

WAIT! PLEASE!
MY MOM WON'T EVER KNOW WHAT HAPPENED TO ME!

RUN, AIMÉE!
OFF WITH EVERYONE'S HEADS!

CHAPTER 10
THE OFFERING
I JUST WANT TO GO HOME.
I MISS MY BED.
I MISS MY MOM.
AND HER GARDEN. SNEAKING HER STRAWBERRIES.

SHTAAHAA! WHAT A BIG COCOON!
NOT A CATERPILLAR. NOT A BUTTERFLY.
ALWAYS TRANSFORMING.
THAT'S HOW I FEEL...
WHAT A BEAUTIFUL WAY TO FEEL.
YOU ARE VERY BEAUTIFUL.
SO ARE YOU.
I DON'T KNOW ABOUT THAT.
YOU WOULD KNOW IF YOU LOOKED.

WAIT!
I JUST...

OKAY TRICKSTER, HERE'S HOPING YOUR WORD IS GOOD.
PAAYEHNSAG, PLEASE ACCEPT THESE GIFTS.
I'M SURE THEY'LL BE HERE ANY MINUTE NOW.

BOOZHOO!

PLEASE, FOLLOW ME.
EHN. MIIGWECH.
WELCOME TO OUR COMMUNITY.
WOW! SO THE STORIES REALLY ARE TRUE.
OF COURSE! ALL STORIES ARE TRUE!

YOU WILL FEAST WITH US!
OH NO, WHAT ABOUT MY PROMISE TO JIIBAYAABOOZ...
DON'T WORRY SO MUCH! IT'LL ALL WORK OUT AS INTENDED. IT ALWAYS DOES!

WE CAN ALL VERY EASILY HEAR YOUR THOUGHTS.

YOU MUST PRACTICE PROTECTING YOUR MIND AND EMOTIONS BEFORE YOU HAVE ANY HOPE OF SURVIVING THE ONE WHO MAKES THE WATER TURN BLACK.

AAMBE!
BE TENDER WITH YOUR MIND AND YOUR HEART.
REMEMBER TO PROTECT YOURSELF AS YOU RETURN TO YOUR FULL SELF.
UNTIL I SEE YOU AGAIN.

CHAPTER 11
THE REFLECTION
FEELS GOOD TO BE BACK TO NORMAL.
WHATEVER "NORMAL" MEANS.
AIMÉE COME CLOSER...
WHO ARE YOU?
I'M YOU.

YOU ALWAYS MAKE MISTAKES.
YOU ALWAYS MESS UP PROTOCOL.
IT'S TOO LATE TO STAND UP FOR YOURSELF.
I'M SORRY.

OH NO!
WHAT...?
TRICKSTER!
NEVER THOUGHT I'D BE SO GLAD TO SEE YOU AGAIN!

DID YOU THINK I'D LET YOU GET MY REVENGE ALL BY YOURSELF?
WELL, I MEAN...
WATCH OUT!

COME AT ME!
WOO, THAT'S COLD!
WHAT SHOULD I DO?!
STAY BACK!

JIIBAYAABOOZ!
DON'T LET YOURSELF GET PULLED INTO THIS. THIS IS MY MESS, NOT YOURS!

I'M COMING FOR YOU!

CHAPTER 12
THE RIVER

WE'RE NOT ALONE!

I HOPE WE WIN THIS FOR JIIBAYAABOOZ...

MIIGWECH FOR CARING FOR ME.
I HATE GETTING WET.

MIIGWECH FOR YOUR HELP, PAAYEHNSAG MINWAA AIMÉE.
MIIGWECH BACK AT YOU. PRETTY SURE I WOULD'VE LOST MY HEAD WITHOUT YOU.
WE BETTER GET YOU OUT OF HERE BEFORE YOU END UP IN COURT AGAIN.
I LIKE MY HEAD WHERE IT IS.

CHAPTER 13
RETURNING
BUT THERE'S TROUBLE BACK THERE TOO...
YOU GET TO GO HOME NOW!
ALWAYS REMEMBER THOSE IN YOUR LIFE WHO ARE GOOD OF HEART.

WEIRD...
I WISH WE COULD HANG OUT TOGETHER AWAY FROM SCHOOL EVERY DAY.
SCHOOL'S NOT ALL BAD.
SAYS THE PERSON WHO DOESN'T GET PICKED ON.
I'M SORRY. THEY'RE REALLY MEAN TO YOU.
YEAH, THEY'RE ALWAYS AFTER AIMÉE TOO.
I DIDN'T KNOW ANYONE EVEN NOTICED.

HEY.
OH, HEY!
HEY, AIMÉE.
I KNOW A GOOD PLACE FROM THE LAST CEREMONY.
WANNA COME WITH ME?
OH, YEAH, OKAY.
WITH GOOD THOUGHTS.
MIIGWECH.

WANT SOME DEMINAN?
MIIGWECH!
HEY, NICE NECKLACE.
HUH?

OH, YEAH, THIS...
IT WAS A GIFT FROM PAAYEHNSAG.
COOL.
WHAT KIND OF OFFERING GETS YOU ONE OF THOSE?

Elizabeth LaPensée (she/they) is an award-winning Anishinaabe, Métis, and Irish writer and illustrator whose work appears in *Moonshot: The Indigenous Comics Collection* series, *Deer Woman: An Anthology*, and more.

KC Oster (he/she/they) is an Ojibwe-Anishinaabe comic artist and illustrator. They live in the Rainy River District of Northwestern Ontario.

Aarin Migiziins (Little Eagle) Dokum ndizhinikaas, Wiikwemkoosing, Wiikwe-mkoong ndo njibaa. (My name is Aarin Dokum and my Nishinaabe noozwin/ Anishinaabe name is Migiziins. I am from Wikwemkoosing, Wikwemikong Ontario, Canada.)